Peter
and the
Bogeyman

Story by Michael Ratnett

Illustrations by June Goulding

BARRON'S

New York

"Don't do that," said Peter's grandad. "The Bogeyman will get you."
"Have you ever seen the Bogeyman, Grandad?" asked Peter.

"Of course," said Peter's grandad. "He's seven feet tall. He's got five arms, and he wears a cape with a hood."

"Just look at the mess you've made!" said Peter's grandma. "It would serve you right if the Bogeyman got you."

"Have you ever seen the Bogeyman, Gran?" asked Peter.

"Certainly not," said Peter's grandma. "I was always too good.
But I know all about him. He sneaks up on naughty children and
scares them stiff. And if that doesn't do any good, he uses his
most powerful spell and turns them into salt. Then he carries them
back to his castle to flavor his soup."

"Have *you* ever seen the Bogeyman, Dad?" asked Peter.
   "There's no such thing as the Bogeyman," said Peter's dad.
"He's just something made up to scare children into being good."

"Yes," said Peter's mom. "There's no such thing. Who's been filling your head with all that nonsense?"

Peter thought and thought about the Bogeyman. And the more
he thought, the more it seemed that if the Bogeyman *was* real,
then it was time that somebody did something about him.

So he made his plans.

On Monday he was quite naughty.

On Tuesday he was very naughty.

On Wednesday he was very, *very* naughty.

And on Thursday he was a complete disgrace!

"The Bogeyman must be coming for me now or never!" he said on Friday.

And that evening, when he went up to bed, he carried a big cardboard box with him.

It was a dark, dark night. Peter waited in bed with his flashlight at his side.

As the town clock struck midnight, the window of Peter's room was raised by a silent hand.

And in climbed a shadowy figure. It was seven feet tall. It had five arms. And it was wearing a hood and cape.

It was the BOGEYMAN!

Peter waited and waited until the Bogeyman was right in the middle of the room. Then he shone the beam of the flashlight straight in his eyes.

"AARGH!" went the Bogeyman, covering his eyes because the light hurt so much. He staggered forward.

Then Peter pulled the rug away, and the Bogeyman fell flat on his back.

"AARGH!" went the Bogeyman, furious at being tripped.
He began to crawl toward Peter.

Peter hurled a bag of flour in the Bogeyman's face.
  SPLAT!

"AARGH!" coughed the Bogeyman, who had never been made
to look so silly before.

Then as he wiped the flour from his eyes, Peter pulled a string, and a great big net dropped over the Bogeyman.

He was trapped!

"AARGH! AARGH! AARGH!" roared the Bogeyman, who was now very, very, *very* angry.

He tore the net to pieces . . .

Then he raised himself up to his full height, and gathered up every last bit of his magic . . .

And with a TERRIBLE yell he threw his most super-duper ten times ordinary strength extra-powerful salt spell right at Peter!

But, quick as a flash, Peter pulled out a mirror and sent the spell bouncing right back at the Bogeyman.
ZAPFIZZPOP!

The Bogeyman instantly turned into a statue of salt!

"And that's the end of you," said Peter.

On Monday, when Peter went to school, he took the Bogeyman statue with him.

He entered it in the Art Competition. Everyone thought that it was very good, and the judges awarded him Second Prize.

His friend Susan came in First with her clay kangaroo, even
though its tail was a bit wobbly.

"Well done," said Peter's mom and dad. "But what is it?"
"It's the Bogeyman," said Peter.

"But there's no such thing," they said.
"Not any more," said Peter.

Peter gave the Bogeyman statue to the school cooks to flavor the children's soup.

And they didn't have to buy any more salt—not for a whole year!